Stage Fright!

SECOND SESSION #7

Stage Fright!

By N. B. Grace

...sed on "Camp Rock," Written by Karin Gist & Regina Hicks and Julie Brown & Paul Brown

DISNEP PRESS

New York

Printed in the United States of America

First Edition
1 3 5 7 9 10 8 6 4 2

Library of Congress Catalog Card Number on file.
ISBN 978-1-4231-1777-3

For more Disney Press fun, visit www.disneybooks.com
Visit DisneyChannel.com

CHAPTER ONE

"Hey, Mom, what's cookin'?" Mitchie Torres said as she dashed into the Camp Rock kitchen.

Her mother, Connie, turned from the stove and grinned at her daughter. "No matter how many times I hear that joke, it never gets old," she said drily. "It's truly amazing."

Mitchie laughed. "I know it's an oldie—but you gotta admit, it's a goody!" She danced over to the refrigerator, her dark brown hair bouncing, and grabbed a carton of orange juice. As she poured herself a glass, she hummed softly.

She still couldn't believe that she was at Camp Rock. And when she thought about all the good friends—such as Caitlyn, Peggy, Lola, and Shane—she had made over the summer, she felt even luckier.

Her spirits were especially high today, because it was a picture-perfect summer morning. The sun was warm, but a cool breeze kept the temperature down. The sky was cloudless and a brilliant blue. Birds were singing cheerfully in the trees. *In fact . . .*

Mitchie cocked her head to listen more closely. It wasn't just birds singing! A few campers who had already finished breakfast were hanging out in the mess hall, practicing a song a cappella. Mitchie nodded to herself as she listened. It was hard to sing without any musical accompaniment and sound good . . . and these singers sounded really good.

Curious, she pushed the kitchen door open and peeked into the dining area. Three girls sitting at a nearby table were the singers. They could have been triplets, Mitchie thought. All three had ponytails (although two of the ponytails were brown and one was blond); all three were wearing identical khaki shorts and white T-shirts; and all three swayed to the beat of the music in a synchronized fashion. As they finished their song, there was a light round of applause from the other campers in the mess hall.

"Awesome job, Torie!" Barron James yelled.

The girl with the blond ponytail smiled and waved a hand in acknowledgment, then said to the other two, "We nailed that one, guys. Do you want to practice 'Sitting on the Dock of the Bay' now?"

Her friends nodded.

"Great," Torie said. "Follow me. . . ."

As they began crooning the classic Otis Redding song, Mitchie closed the door.

"I guess we got some new campers," she said.

Her mother squirted some soap into the sink full of hot water. "Yes, I heard Brown talking about that last night," she said as she plunged a dirty pan into the sink. "Or maybe I should say, I heard him groovin' to an extremely enthusiastic beat about how cool it was that he could arrange for some kids to arrive a few days late for the session."

Mitchie grinned at her mother's wry tone. Brown Cesario had retired from a long career in the music business to become the director of Camp Rock, and his high spirits and abundant energy definitely kept the place rockin'. Not to mention his endless tales of musicians he had known and his unique way of working music into any conversation.

"Well, it doesn't sound like they'll have a

4

hard time catching up," Mitchie observed, nodding toward the mess hall, where the girls were finishing up their song with some smooth and soulful vocals. "Hey, do you need some help with drying?"

"Thanks, honey," Connie said with a warm smile. "But you need to eat your breakfast first. You know, breakfast is—"

"The most important meal of the day. I know, I know!" Mitchie finished her mother's sentence. "Okay, let me finish my nutritious breakfast and then I'll have the energy I need to come back in here and help out."

A few minutes later, Mitchie had filled her plate with scrambled eggs. As she was nabbing a slice of toast, she looked around the canteen for a seat.

Her best friend, Caitlyn Gellar, was nowhere to be seen. Mitchie grinned. Bunking in the same cabin, Mitchie had discovered that Caitlyn was a real night owl who loved to stay up late talking or practicing the guitar or learning a new song. Last night, she'd been reading a new novel that she said she just couldn't put down. Even as Mitchie had drifted off to sleep, Caitlyn's mini-reading light was still glowing in the dark cabin. And now Mitchie had a feeling that her friend was probably willing to miss breakfast—despite its *obvious* importance!—in order to get a little extra sleep.

As Mitchie's eyes continued to scan the room, a hint of disappointment clouded her good mood. When she stopped to figure out what had caused the dip in her spirits, she realized that she'd been hoping not just to see Caitlyn. She had also been hoping to see Shane Gray.

Not that she didn't see quite a lot of him. In fact, she still couldn't believe she was friends with the lead singer of the super-famous band Connect Three—who also happened to be Brown's nephew. But then again, Camp Rock had been nothing if not surprising. Their friendship was another amazing thing that had happened to Mitchie there.

Even though Shane wasn't in the mess hall, Mitchie was certain to see him later. Right now, she had to hurry up and eat so that she could go help her mom. Mitchie took a seat in a secluded corner, where she was half hidden behind a rolling equipment trunk that had been wheeled into the room for that afternoon's acoustic set. She realized that she was actually pleased to have a little time to herself so she could think about something that had been troubling her.

She had been working on a song all week. It had started off well, but then she got stuck after finishing one verse. Every line she had written after that seemed forced. Every note she tried sounded false.

Part of her knew that she should put the song aside and work on something else.

Often, when she did that, she came back to the problem song and found that the solution was obvious, as if her mind had been working on it while she was busily thinking other thoughts.

But she felt *so close* to figuring out how to write this song! She didn't want to give up. Mitchie felt as if the song already existed somewhere just beyond her grasp, shimmering in the future. If only she could reach out and grab it . . .

She tapped her fingers on the table as she went over the lyrics she had written. She forgot her disappointment about not finding Caitlyn or Shane in the mess hall. This alone time was giving her a chance to concentrate—that is until her thoughts were interrupted by a voice behind her.

"I can't believe I'm actually here at Camp Rock!" a girl said.

Mitchie turned her head slightly as she recognized the voice of Torie, one of the new girls. She and her friends had clearly gone back for second helpings and regrouped at a table on the other side of the equipment trunk.

"I keep pinching myself to make sure I'm not dreaming," one of the other girls gushed. Her voice was high-pitched, and she spoke very quickly. Probably just excited, Mitchie thought. And maybe a *teeny* bit over-caffeinated.

"I know *just* what you mean, Jessie," the third girl chimed in. She had a honeyed Southern drawl. "So many famous people got their starts here. There might even be a chance for someone like me, li'l ole Sally Jo from Harriman, Tennessee!"

Mitchie smiled to herself. She had felt exactly that same way when she had arrived at Camp Rock—and she still did. She toyed with the idea of getting up and intro-ducing herself to the threesome. They clearly didn't know she was sitting right behind them, and eavesdropping—even by accident—wasn't a cool thing to do. Plus, she could welcome them to camp, answer any questions they had, and maybe make a few more friends. . . .

But then Torie spoke again, and Mitchie found herself glued to her seat.

"*Anything* can happen here," Torie said confidently. "I mean, just look at Mitchie Torres!"

"Exactly!" Jessie cried, still gushing. "She's one of Camp Rock's stars! Did you guys hear that song she was singing last night at the jam session? She actually wrote it! All by herself! And it was awesome!"

"That's true," Sally Jo said. "She was new here not that long ago, just like us, and look how far she's come."

Mitchie relaxed a little. Whoever said that eavesdroppers never hear anything good about themselves was clearly wrong, she thought smugly.

Then she frowned as she remembered exactly which song she had performed last night. It *was* good . . . but it was a pretty old song, one that she had written months ago and then tweaked a little at camp. It probably still needed work, if she was honest with herself.

That reminded her, once more, of the song she was struggling with now. Her spirits drooped again.

Maybe I should try working on the chorus, she thought, frowning in concentration. If I nail that, the rest of the verses might come more easily . . .

But once again, her thoughts were interrupted by Torie. "Oh, yeah, Mitchie's a great songwriter," she said. "I really admire her talent. But let's face it, talent only takes you so far in the music business."

Mitchie's frown deepened.

Jessie sounded puzzled. "What do you mean?"

"Just that Mitchie's really lucky she knows Shane," Torie said in a practical voice. "Making that kind of connection is pure gold. That's the other thing that Camp Rock offers. We should make the most of it and do all the networking we can while we're here."

"I guess you're right," Jessie said.

"Like my daddy says, it's all about who you know," Sallie Jo agreed.

Mitchie felt a strange emotion surge through her. She wasn't exactly angry . . . after all, the girls had complimented her songwriting. And she wasn't exactly embarrassed . . . after all, she was proud to be Shane's friend.

Still . . . she had come to Camp Rock because she wanted to be an artist.

But it sounded as if Torie and her friends thought that it was enough for Mitchie to be known as just Shane's friend.

"Hey, it's almost time for the hip-hop

seminar," Torie said. "Come on, let's go, or we'll be late."

Mitchie heard the sound of the three girls cleaning their table and taking their trays over to the metal cart where campers left their dirty plates and silverware. She leaned back just far enough to watch them as they left the mess hall. Then she counted to ten, just to be sure they were really gone, before standing up and heading over to the cart herself.

Once she placed her own plate on it, she sighed and started pushing it toward the kitchen. If she hurried, she'd have time to help her mom wash these dishes and still make it to the songwriting workshop that Brown was teaching in an hour.

Keep your eyes on the prize, Mitchie, she told herself. You know why you're here—to learn about your art. Who cares what a few new girls think?

But still, as she stepped outside a moment

later to scrape some dried egg into the garbage, she couldn't help but notice that the sky had clouded up, and the sun no longer seemed to shine quite so brightly.

CHAPTER TWO

"Hey, Mitchie, want to grab some lunch?" Caitlyn called out.

Turning, Mitchie smiled as she saw her friend walking down the path toward her. Brown's songwriting seminar had been great, but, as usual, he had gone fifteen minutes over schedule. No one minded—Brown was a teacher who could inspire you and make you laugh at the same time—but Mitchie was definitely feeling some hunger pangs.

"You bet," she said as Caitlyn caught up with her. "In fact, let's hurry! Mom's making sloppy joes today, and you know those always go fast."

They quickened their pace as they saw other campers heading for the mess hall. Inside there was a buzz of activity. Everyone was lining up for food, laughing and joking around, and even singing snatches of songs as they waited.

Mitchie smiled at the sight. All the campers were so happy to be at Camp Rock— it was hard to find people in a negative mood, even when they were hungry and standing in a long line. Well . . . *almost* all the campers.

"What is holding up lunch?" a voice complained behind Mitchie. "We're having sloppy joes *again*? They're so heavy, I find it hard to perform. I hope that at least today's salad will be good, since that's all I'll be able to eat."

Sighing, Mitchie turned to face the complainer—Tess Tyler. "The salad today is tuna *niçoise*," she said. "I can testify that it's delicious . . . and I promise it won't weigh you down."

Tess smirked. "Thanks for the scoop," she said a little too sweetly. "I guess that's one of the perks of being the cook's daughter—you get all kinds of inside info about what's going to be served."

Mitchie's face grew warm. Inwardly, she was mad at herself for blushing. She wasn't ashamed of her mother—far from it! But Tess's little dig reminded Mitchie of how she had lied about her mother's job when she first came to Camp Rock . . . something she wasn't proud of. But at the time, Mitchie had just wanted desperately to impress Tess—the daughter of pop star T.J. Tyler and therefore total rock royalty.

She sensed that Tess knew her dart had hit home, so Mitchie resolved not to snap back.

Instead, she gritted her teeth and said, "I sure do. For instance, I also happen to know that we're having a superawesome dessert. It's so wonderful that I've been sworn to secrecy! No matter what you do or say, I will not reveal the true nature of today's sweet surprise—"

"Oh, come on, Mitchie, don't tease us," another voice said behind them, causing Mitchie's heart to race.

Tess's head swung around, and a huge smile replaced her scowl. She flipped her blond hair over her shoulder. "Hi, Shane!" she said, taking in the handsome pop star. "I can't wait for tonight's bonfire! I'm sure you're going to be the star of the night . . . as usual!"

"Oh, stop," Shane said, waving one hand dismissively. "My legend is greatly exaggerated."

Caitlyn laughed. "Don't try to act modest," she teased. "Your reputation precedes you."

Mitchie looked between her friends. What were they talking about? "Um, what legend is that?" she asked aloud. "And more importantly, what reputation?"

By this time they had reached the door of the mess hall. Shane held it open for the three girls. As Tess passed him, she said, "Oh, that's right, you wouldn't know, would you, Mitchie . . . since this is your first year at Camp Rock."

As she said this, she smiled up at Shane, as if they were sharing something special from having attended the camp in the past.

Before Mitchie could respond, however, Caitlyn broke in. "Tonight's the annual Scary Story Bonfire," she explained. "It's a Camp Rock tradition."

Mitchie nodded. "Right," she said. "I read the flyers that were posted in B-Note. So?"

"Soooo, Shane just happens to be the best at telling scary stories!" Tess said, bringing the attention back to herself. "I still shiver when I think of that one story you told about the vampire who pretended to be a hiker so he could find his next victims on the trail . . . ooooh!" She gave a theatrical shiver.

Caitlyn caught Mitchie's eye and gave a tiny wink. "Yeah, Shane managed to spook everyone," she said. "Even Barron and Sander screamed—"

"What are you saying about me?" interrupted Barron, who had overheard Caitlyn. He was grinning. "Are you claiming that Sander and I were in any way unnerved by Shane's little horror story?"

As if on cue, Sander Loya bounced up to them, a smoothie in hand. "No way!" he cried. "We weren't scared at all! If we screamed—"

"It was because we felt Shane's performance needed some sound effects," Barron finished.

"If we jumped out of our seats—"

"It was because we wanted to add to

the overall *ambience*," Barron said.

"And if it looked like our hands were shaking—"

"That was just an optical illusion," Barron finished. "Firelight is deceptive, you know."

Everyone laughed. Shane shook his head as Barron gave him a high five.

"These guys are just kidding around," Shane said, turning to Mitchie. "Believe me, when you're sitting around a bonfire at night in the middle of the woods, *any* story sounds frightening."

Tess shook her head and placed her hands on her hips. "Oh, I don't believe that," she said. "Why don't you try telling us a story over lunch? I bet you'll be able to terrify us, even in broad daylight!"

Shane held up his hands and backed away. "No, no, no," he said, chuckling. "I've got to save my best stuff for tonight. Sorry."

By the time they had all filled their plates with food, four other campers had approached Shane and said how much they were looking forward to hearing his story that night.

By the time they found seats together at a table, three campers had waved to Shane and shouted, "Can't wait for tonight!" and "Oooh, I'm scared already!"

And by the time Mitchie had taken her first bite of sloppy joe, she was intensely curious about the evening ahead.

"How did the Scary Story Bonfire become a Camp Rock tradition anyway?" she asked. "It's not very musical."

"I'm glad you asked that, Mitchie," a hearty voice boomed.

She turned to see Brown, who was holding a tray piled high with desserts, walking up to their table.

"Is your sweet tooth bothering you again, Brown?" Shane asked, deadpan.

"Oh, you bet," Brown answered as he took a seat at the head of the table. "One of these days, I've got to get the dentist to pull it. But for now—" He raised a brownie in a salute. "Cheers!"

After taking a big bite, he said to Mitchie, "The tradition started years ago at what was supposed to be a perfectly ordinary camp bonfire. But on that particular night, I began telling a story . . . a story so frightening, so hair-raisingly scary, so chilling, that every camper who heard it could never forget it, no matter how hard they tried!"

Mitchie, Shane, and Caitlyn laughed at the overly dramatic spooky voice he was using; Barron and Sander rolled their eyes; and even Tess smiled slightly.

"So many people retold my story over the next year that it became—if I do say so myself—somewhat of a legend," Brown went on. "By the time the next summer rolled around, campers were clamoring to hear it again. Naturally, I didn't want to hog the spotlight—"

"Of course not," Shane murmured drily. He traded a knowing smile with Mitchie.

Brown pretended not to hear his nephew. "So I insisted that other people tell their stories instead," he said. "They did—and wouldn't you know, every story was scarier than the one before! Everyone had such a great time that we decided to make the scary-story-telling bonfire an annual event. *And* I've never repeated my extraspecial story since that very first bonfire. It's part of the tradition. Not even Shane here—or Nate or Jason, for that matter, has heard it." He paused and smiled at his nephew. He knew Shane and his bandmates were close and had had their fair share of Camp Rock summers. Brown also knew that if Shane had heard the story, the boys would have, too. He took a big bite of ice cream and waggled his eyebrows at the campers before adding, "You know what they say—start the ball rolling and then stand back and let others keep it going."

Mitchie raised an eyebrow and grinned at Brown. "So, I have to ask," she said. "Can you tell us the story now? I'd love to hear it."

"That would be great!" Caitlyn agreed, as Barron and Sander whistled their approval.

"Well, I don't know," Brown said. "I mean, I've *never* repeated that performance since that very first bonfire . . ."

"But we're not at a bonfire now," Tess pointed out, looking interested in spite of her attempts to play every situation cool. "And it sounds like an awesome story. . . ."

Brown looked at the six eager faces around the table. He hesitated, then shrugged. He knew that when the fans demanded an encore, a good performer never denied them. "Sure, why not?" he said, smiling. "Might as well get the party started!"

CHAPTER THREE

Within a few minutes, Brown's eager audience of six had grown much larger. The news that Brown was going to tell his legendary story had traveled fast.

Brown now had an audience of eager campers gathered around him. Reveling in the attention, he took a seat and began telling his story as the campers ate lunch.

"I know you guys think that ghosts only

haunt old mansions," he began. "But I've actually seen a ghost face-to-face—and it was in a place you'd never, ever expect."

"Let me guess . . . it was in a backstage dressing room," Barron wisecracked. "Late at night, after three encores, when you were hanging out with the Stones—"

"No," Brown said somberly. He looked from one face to another, his expression very serious. "The ghost I saw was haunting a tour bus!"

"No way!" Mitchie cried. "When was this?"

"Oh, back in the seventies," Brown said with a dismissive wave of his hand. "Before any of you guys were even born. I was touring with a band called the Purple Prunes—"

"The Purple Prunes?" Shane repeated. He was clearly trying not to snicker, but his brown eyes were bright with laughter. "You're kidding, right?"

"No, I'm not," Brown said, pretending to be

offended. "And the name made perfect sense at the time."

Shane raised his eyebrows skeptically. "Oh, yeah?"

"Yeah!" Brown insisted. "It was *the seventies*, mate."

Caitlyn tilted her head. "Actually, that band sounds familiar."

Brown nodded encouragingly. "Spoken like someone who knows her music history," he said. "Now if you will all let me continue with my story, you'll find out exactly *why* Purple Prunes rings a bell for some."

"Well, go on," Tess ordered, her curiosity getting the best of her. She squeezed onto the end of a bench in order to be as close as possible to Brown, forcing Caitlyn to scoot over. "What happened?"

"Well, back in the day, up-and-coming bands had pretty tough touring schedules," he said. "We'd play a set in Columbus, get on the bus and head to Dayton, then Lexington, then Nashville, then Memphis, and every little podunk town in between night after night. We'd try to sleep on the bus, but it was hard to nod off—and I always woke up with a stiff neck. Everybody was always tired. One time, we figured out that we spent ten times as many hours rolling along the highway as we did onstage! Let me tell you, mates, it got to the point where we hated that old bus with a passion."

He leaned forward and lowered his voice. His handsome face grew still more serious and his accented voice thickened. "And then one night, we had an experience none of us would ever forget. It was a little past midnight, and we were driving down a small country road out West. I think we were somewhere in Nevada, headed for a little rundown club called The Thirsty Buffalo. We had just rounded a sharp corner when the driver slammed on the brakes and we screeched to a halt.

"As you can imagine, we were all pretty confused. Everyone looked out the windows to see what was up. I thought maybe there had been a wreck or something. But what we saw was a beautiful young woman, dressed in a fancy black party dress and carrying a guitar case. She was standing by the road in the middle of nowhere, pale and forlorn looking, like she'd just about given up on being rescued."

He paused to take a sip of his iced tea, his eyes twinkling over the rim of his glass as he took in the reaction of his listeners.

Barron's fork was suspended halfway to his mouth. Tess's eyes were open wide. Mitchie and Caitlyn were holding their breath. Only Shane had enough presence of mind to ask the question everybody was thinking:

"So what happened next?"

"Glad you asked." Brown leaned forward. "When the bus stopped, the driver opened the door and asked the young woman if she needed help. She said that she had been waiting an hour for a lift and would be very grateful if we could take her down the road to The Thirsty Buffalo."

"And you did, right?" Sanders interrupted.

"Of course," Brown said. "She climbed aboard, and we made room for her. Naturally, we all got to talking. She told us that she was a singer and that we could call her Lil. She said that she performed all over the country, but she had started her career at The Thirsty Buffalo. As we kept rolling down the road, she told us about all the cities she'd visited and all the memories she'd made. One of the Prunes, Joanie, bonded with Lil right away, since they were both singers—although Joanie was pretty much a complete unknown at that point. It was a long ride, and I noticed that Lil was huddling with Joanie at one point, giving her advice, I guess. Then we finally got to The Thirsty Buffalo. We all stood up to stretch, grab our jackets, that sort of thing. But when we turned around to see if Lil needed anything . . . she was gone!"

Mitchie and Caitlyn exchanged glances. Shane shrugged. Tess wasn't as quiet. "So she went out the bus door before you guys," she said. "What's the big deal?"

Brown looked intensely at each camper in turn and then shook his head. "There was absolutely no way for her to get past us without anyone seeing her," he insisted. "Absolutely. Positively. No. Way. It really spooked us. When we finally went in to the club, the owner overheard us talking about Lil, wondering where she might have gone.

"He came up to us and said, 'Oh, you picked up the Woman in Black!'

"Of course we were confused," Brown continued. "My bandmate Joe said, 'What do you mean? We picked up a girl named Lil.'"

"'That's right,' the owner replied, 'The

Woman in Black—Lillian Wylie. She sang here fifty years ago, when the club was called Rose's Grille. She was a real big star in her day, at least in these parts. Some people even said she would have made a record one day and become a national star. But then . . ."

Brown paused dramatically.

After the silence had stretched out for almost a minute, Caitlyn finally asked, "But then, what?"

"But then she died in a car crash, right around the spot where we picked her up," Brown finished. "And ever since, she's been said to haunt the place where the accident happened. But here's the thing: not everyone could see her. In fact, she *only* appeared to musicians."

"Creepy," Mitchie said softly, shivering.

"No, no, it's wasn't creepy! It was cool!" Brown argued. "See, the only musicians who saw her were the ones who were going to make it big! Any band in the world would

33

have been thrilled to have the Woman in Black on their tour bus."

There was a short silence as the campers absorbed the story. Then Shane pointed out the obvious. "But the Purple Prunes broke up and were never heard of again."

"Ah, but I didn't tell you who our lead singer was," Brown said smugly. "None other than Joanie Jameson!"

That got Tess's attention. Her head swung around and her gaze focused intensely on Brown. "*The* Joanie Jameson?" she asked. "I thought she was always a solo artist."

A small murmur ran around the table. Everyone knew about Joanie Jameson, a singer/songwriter who had recorded dozens of albums, won numerous Grammys, and now served as an inspiration to a new generation of artists.

"Nope," Brown said, looking, if possible, even more self-satisfied. "Her very first job was with the Prunes. When the band broke up, she went off on her own—and the rest, as they say, is history."

"Wow," Mitchie said in a hushed voice.

"Yeah," Brown said. "The Woman in Black started Joanie on her way to becoming a superstar." He took a final sip of tea and added, "Later, of course, Joanie hired all the Prunes for her backup band, so you could say they made it big, too. I was the only one who couldn't join them, because by that time I was on the road with Aerosmith. Which reminds me of another really cool story, by the way . . ."

CHAPTER FOUR

Mitchie joined everyone else in applauding Brown's story (and convincing him to leave the Aerosmith story, which they had *all* heard several times, for another day). Then she caught sight of the new girl, Torie, sitting at the next table. She was clapping, too, but as she did, her gaze shifted back and forth between Mitchie and Shane. There was a knowing look on her face.

Suddenly, Mitchie felt self-conscious. She stood and picked up her tray.

"Hey, where are you going?" Shane asked. "You haven't even had dessert."

"I think I'll skip the sweets today," Mitchie said. "I, uh, promised my mom that I'd help her out in the kitchen."

Shane looked surprised, but he nodded. "Sure," he said. "Hey, how about I give you a hand?"

Mitchie glanced over to the next table. Torie was staring at them, her eyes gleaming with interest.

"Um, thanks but . . . I don't want to make you late for your workshop this afternoon," she said.

"Mitchie?" Shane put his hand on her arm and looked deep into her eyes. "Are you all right? You seem a little down."

Mitchie mustered a bright smile and returned his look as directly as she dared. It was hard not to get distracted by his kind eyes or warm hand, and she needed to stay focused—there was no way she was going to give Torie any ammunition. "Of *course* I'm all right," she said. "I'm just in a hurry. I have to help my mom make five dozen muffins before I can go to the rockin' rhythm seminar! Blueberry muffins! Which are much harder than plain muffins, I'll have you know—"

"Okay, okay," he said, laughing and throwing up his hands in surrender. "Go forth and make blueberry muffins! I'll see you tonight at the bonfire, right?"

"Absolutely," she said, relieved. After all, how could she admit to him that she was afraid if she ever became famous it would be because of their friendship? Shane might think that she didn't want to be friends with him . . . which was *so* far from the truth! Their friendship was too important, too precious to destroy over silly overthinking. Still . . .

She watched him walk away and sighed as

Caitlyn headed in her direction, carrying their dirty plates.

Cocking one eyebrow at Mitchie, Caitlyn asked, "What's wrong, Mitchie?"

Mitchie opened her mouth to answer, then saw Torie standing by the dessert table. She was eyeing a slice of chocolate cake and clearly doing her best to overhear Mitchie's conversation.

"Nothing at all," Mitchie said loudly. "Hey, Caitlyn! Want to help me mix up some blueberry-muffin batter?"

An hour later, Mitchie and Caitlyn had popped the last tray in the oven and were sitting down to enjoy a snack of piping hot muffins from the first batch. Mitchie cut her muffin in half, slathered butter on it, and took a big bite.

"So . . . give," Caitlyn demanded as she waited for her own muffin to cool off. "You've been really distracted today. What's going on?" She had noticed that her friend and bunkmate had been surprisingly quiet while they baked. She hadn't even laughed when Caitlyn made fun of Tess's scared expression at lunch.

Mitchie was glad that her mouth was full. While she chewed and swallowed, she could also think. By the time she was ready to answer, Caitlyn was giving her a suspicious look, even as she nibbled at the delicious crust of her muffin.

"Okay, I'll tell you," Mitchie began. "But first, you have to know that this is *totally* not a big deal."

Caitlyn lifted her eyebrows in amusement. "Oh, *yeah*," she said. "Not a big deal. You just look strung tighter than a guitar. Obviously you are not upset at all."

Mitchie made a face and flicked some leftover batter at her friend. Caitlyn laughed even though the batter hit her nose. Mitchie reluctantly grinned back.

Then she went ahead and repeated what she had overheard Torie and her friends say about her.

". . . and I know it shouldn't upset me, but it really, really . . . well . . . *upset* me," she finished. "You can understand why, can't you?"

Caitlyn nodded slowly. "Yeah. I *guess* so. . . ."

A small frown appeared on Mitchie's face. "What do you mean, you guess so?" she asked. "It's so obvious why I'm upset."

"Ri-ight," Caitlyn said. "Totally obvious. But maybe you could just spell it out for me?"

Mitchie threw her hands in the air in frustration. "I don't want everyone to think that I'm using Shane!"

"Oh, come on, no one could think that!" Caitlyn cried adamantly, finally understanding.

"Well, thanks." Mitchie relaxed a little at Caitlyn's protest. Still, she felt troubled. "But what about my songs? I want people to judge them on their own merit. I don't want anyone to give me a pass because they're trying to get in good with Shane. And I don't want anyone to think that any success I do—or don't—achieve is because I'm friends or not friends with him. There's no way to know what will happen once camp is over. He is going to be on tour with Connect Three or recording or whatever, and I have to go home and back to school. And who knows if I ever will write another good song."

Mitchie paused to catch her breath. Caitlyn rolled her eyes and took another big bite of muffin. Her friend was being a *bit* overdramatic. Still, she could sympathize with how Mitchie was feeling. "Mitchie, you are—" She stopped and held up a finger to show that she had to pause while she finished chewing her food. When she could speak again, she said, "You are a songwriter, heart and soul. Anyone can see that."

Mitchie gave her a grateful smile, but she shook her head. "My *friends* can see that," she said. "And I thank you! But people who don't know me . . . I'm starting to realize that they're going to make all kinds of judgments about me. And I'm not sure what to do about that."

"Well, that's simple," Caitlyn said.

"It is?" Mitchie cast a hopeful look at her friend.

"Sure," Caitlyn went on. "The thing you do is . . . nothing."

"Oh." Mitchie slumped over the counter, her chin in her hands. "Thanks a bunch."

"No, really," her friend insisted. "You can't control what people think about you, so you might as well not even try. All you can do is make sure that you're true to yourself. Then it doesn't matter what anyone else thinks."

"I know you're right," Mitchie said with a sigh. It was good advice, she thought. It was exactly the advice she would have given Caitlyn if their roles were reversed.

So why, she wondered, did she still feel so worried?

"**P**sst! Caitlyn!"

"Aaah!" Caitlyn was walking down a shady path toward her cabin when she heard the whisper emerging from a large bush to her right. She couldn't help it—she jumped and gave a little scream.

"Who's there?" she demanded.

The branches moved back and forth, the leaves rustled, and then Shane stepped out into the open. He glanced up and down the path to make sure they were alone.

"It's just me," he said, grinning. "Sorry I scared you."

She shot him a scorching look. "You didn't scare me," she replied quickly. "You *surprised* me. I'm not used to hearing bushes talk to me."

"Point taken." He nodded, still smiling.

Then his expression turned serious. "Listen, can I talk to you for a second? In private?"

Caitlyn raised her eyebrows in surprise, but she nodded. "Sure."

"Follow me." Shane held back part of the bush, revealing a hidden path, and he stepped into the woods.

Caitlyn followed him until they reached a large rock at the edge of the lake. Shane sat down and gestured for her to join him.

"What's up?" she asked. "Why all the secrecy?"

"I just don't want anyone to overhear us," he explained. He paused and ran a hand through his dark hair. "I wanted to ask you if something's wrong with Mitchie. She's seemed a little . . . I don't know, *sad* recently, and I know you two are best friends, so . . ."

His voice trailed off and he sat watching her, his dark eyes expectant.

Caitlyn hesitated. She and Mitchie *were* good friends—which meant, of course, that they kept each other's secrets. But friends also helped each other out—and if Mitchie was worried about how people saw her friendship with Shane, well, was there any way that Shane could help with that? On the other hand, Mitchie wouldn't want Shane to think that she regretted their friendship. . . . Caitlyn wrinkled her forehead as she tried to think this through.

Shane was watching her closely. "You don't have to tell me if you don't want to," he said. "I just want to help Mitchie if I can."

"Well, um, some of what she told me is kind of private," Caitlyn said. "But I guess I *can* tell you that she's a little worried about her songwriting."

"Why?" Shane looked shocked. "She's a great songwriter. And she works so hard at it. She'll just keep improving, I'm sure of it."

"Yeah, well . . ." Caitlyn tried to think of how to explain Mitchie's worries to Shane without mentioning that he was a big part of those worries. "It's not so much her talent. It's more whether people will see her as an artist, and not just someone who's trying to get famous."

"Oh." Shane gazed out over the water and thought about that for a moment. "Well, she's right to be thinking about that," he said, so softly that he seemed to be talking to himself. "It's easy to get caught up in all the celebrity nonsense."

And *you* would know all about that, Caitlyn thought.

After all, Shane's record label had sent him back to Camp Rock for the summer after he had thrown one too many temper tantrums as the lead singer of Connect Three. At camp, he had found himself—and his voice—again, but the experience was clearly fresh in his mind.

He turned to look directly into Caitlyn's eyes. "You're thinking that I would know, right?" he said teasingly.

She blushed scarlet, embarrassed that he had guessed her thoughts so easily. "No, no, that wasn't even in my mind," she began, but he waved her protests away with a grin.

"If it wasn't, it should have been," he said. "But listen, I'm glad you told me this. I think I can figure out a way to help Mitchie realize that she's got nothing to worry about."

"Really?" Caitlyn looked doubtful. "That would be great, but I have to warn you: words won't be enough to convince her."

He nodded, his expression sly. "You're absolutely right," he agreed. "But I just had the beginning of an idea. If I can work out the details, I think I'll get Mitchie to believe it with all her heart."

CHAPTER FIVE

There was still a little light in the sky as Mitchie and Caitlyn strolled down the path to the location of the campfire that night. Mitchie glanced through the trees at the horizon, where a faint line of pink and gold still remained from the sunset.

Despite her earlier worries, she felt her heart lift. There was something about sitting around a roaring fire with good friends that was both exciting and comforting. And tonight's campfire would be all new to her—she had never had a chance to attend one of Camp Rock's scary storytelling sessions.

Turning her attention from the sky, she glanced at Caitlyn. "So, are you going to tell a story tonight?"

Caitlyn laughed. "Me? No way. I'd rather listen to everyone else and have a good time being frightened."

Mitchie raised one eyebrow. "Are the stories really *that* spooky?"

"Well, no," Caitlyn admitted. "But sitting out in the woods in the dark . . . it's easy for your imagination to get out of control. That's part of the fun."

By the time all the campers had arrived, grabbed some snacks from the picnic baskets that Mitchie's mom had sent down, and found seats, the last of the light had disappeared and the first stars were twinkling in the night sky.

Taking a seat next to Caitlyn, Mitchie took a bite of a chocolate-chip cookie and gazed around at all the familiar faces. Everyone looks a little different in the firelight, she thought. And the dancing flames are casting weird shadows that make the trees and bushes seem almost alive. And did it just get a little windier?

Stop that! she told herself sternly as goose-bumps appeared on her arms. Letting your imagination get a little out of control can be fun, but you're ready to scream before the first story has even started!

At that moment, Shane walked out of the shadows to sit beside her on one of the logs that were serving as benches. Despite herself, she jumped just a little bit at his sudden appearance.

"Hey," he said, his eyes filled with concern. "Are you cold?"

Mitchie realized that she had been rubbing her arms. "Oh, no, not really," she said.

His concern vanished and he grinned. "You're not scared already, are you?" he asked. "The show hasn't even started."

"Of course not!" Mitchie tried to sound confident, but she could tell by his teasing glance that she hadn't succeeded.

"Here." Shane handed her another cookie. "Cookies give you courage. And don't worry," he said with a wink. "I'll stay right here beside you."

Mitchie smiled, feeling much happier, even though she hadn't been scared, not really. . . .

Then she saw Torie out of the corner of her eye. The new girl was looking at Mitchie and whispering to a girl next to her. Mitchie lifted her chin slightly and took a defiant bite of cookie. Caitlyn was right. Mitchie couldn't help what Torie thought about her or her friendship with Shane . . . and she wasn't going to let Torie's earlier comments ruin the bonfire for her. After all, this was a once-in-a-summer opportunity.

She deliberately turned her head so that she could no longer see Torie.

"So," she said to Shane, "who's going to tell the first story?"

"Ladies and gentlemen, boys and girls, please do not be alarmed," Brown said as he stood up to get the entertainment started. "The stories you hear tonight will be frightening, unnerving, maybe even shocking . . ."

"Oooh." Torie and her two friends pretended to shiver, looking delighted.

"Don't worry," Brown said, waving at them reassuringly. "After all, none of the stories are true—"

He looked around at the faces ringing the bonfire and winked. "Or *are* they?" he added in a deliberately spooky voice.

This was greeted with good-natured hoots from the campers. Brown grinned. "Laugh now," he said. "We'll see how you feel after you've heard a few of tonight's terrifying tales! First up . . . Barron James!"

Everybody cheered and clapped as Barron stood up and took a bow. "Thanks," he said. "Now don't get too comfortable or believe Brown too much. My story was handed down in my family from my grandfather to my father and then to me. And I can tell you for a fact that this really happened."

"Nice try, Barron," Andy Hosten, one of Barron's friends, called out. "But you can't scare us."

Barron gave him a sly smile. "Really?" he said. "Well, let's just see shall we . . ."

He sat back down on his log and leaned forward. As he began to tell his story, the firelight flickered on his face. "My grandfather was just a little boy when one summer day his mother told him to go out and weed the garden," he began. "Grandpa Joe did as he was told, but he was a little nervous. You see, the family farm sat on land that had been settled by people who had moved into the area a hundred years before. The garden was on a section of land that had been used as a burial ground. Of course, his parents had been told that all the buried bodies had been moved before the land was sold for farming . . . but Grandpa Joe still felt weird when he was out there picking tomatoes or hoeing the ground."

"Oooh." Tess shivered, more mocking than sincere. "Gardening! This is worse than any horror movie, Barron!"

There were a few chuckles around the fire. Barron smiled and shrugged. "But isn't this how all scary stories start?" he asked. "With a seemingly ordinary day, a seemingly ordinary chore—"

"And a seemingly obvious plot twist," Peggy Dupree interrupted, a teasing note in her voice. "Come on, I'm guessing that there's at least one body still buried in the garden, Barron. Am I right?"

He pointed to her and grinned. "You got it!" he said, undeterred by the skepticism. "In fact, Grandpa Joe had only been hoeing a few minutes when he saw something unusual appear in the dirt. It was a fleshy object, about two inches long. He picked it up and brushed the dirt off. That's when he realized—"

Barron raised his voice slightly and said in a spooky voice, "It was a *human toe!*"

"Ooooh!"

"Gross!"

"Yuck!"

As the campers groaned and laughed, Mitchie caught Shane's eye and grinned. It figured that Barron would be a great storyteller; he had a definite flair for the dramatic—as evidenced by his always-creative dance moves.

"So far, I feel more grossed out than

scared," Shane whispered to her. "I mean, come on . . . a big toe?"

"Shhh," Mitchie whispered back. "Barron's just getting started."

They turned back to watch Barron as he continued with his story. "Grandpa didn't like touching that big toe, but he also didn't want to leave it out there in the yard. So he took it back to the house and showed it to his mother. As one might expect, it worried her, so she told him to put it on the ground outside the kitchen door and that they would figure out what to do with it later when his father got home."

Barron stopped to take a sip out of his water bottle. "Well, Grandpa Joe was a little surprised that she seemed so calm. But he thought maybe it would all be okay. Still, he had a hard time enjoying his dinner that night," he went on. "And it was his favorite meal, too! Chicken and dumplings! But he choked down every bite, his mind constantly turning to that toe, sitting on the ground outside. It made him feel nervous for some reason. But then his mother served chocolate cake for dessert, and he finally forgot about it."

"I can tell where you got your appetite, Barron!" Andy yelled.

"You're right." Barron laughed. "I've always said my passion for pie was hereditary. But enough about me. Guess what happened next?"

"Hmmm . . . just a guess—the ghost of the toe started haunting them?" Shane suggested.

"Very funny," Barron said. "No, my grandpa Joe went to bed."

Peggy yawned. She was ready for more. "And then what? He had a good night's sleep?"

"As a matter of fact," Barron said, "no."

"Here it comes," Shane said, grinning. "The big finish."

Barron smiled slightly as he took another sip of water. "Grandpa Joe did doze off, but then"—Barron's face got serious as he looked around at the circle of listeners—"suddenly, he woke up. His heart was thumping wildly, although he didn't know why. He tried to remain calm, listening hard to see what had awakened him. At first, he heard only the usual sounds of the night: a tree branch scratching against the window, the wind rattling a loose shutter, a clock chiming twelve from the living room downstairs. And then . . ."

Barron lowered his voice. "He heard foot-steps walking across the floor downstairs! They were slow, dragging footsteps . . . and they were heading toward the stairs—and his room!

"Grandpa Joe held his breath. He knew that his mom and dad were asleep in their bedroom. He could hear his dad snoring and his mom talking in her sleep. So who else was in the house? And why was the intruder heading for the stairs?"

Mitchie glanced around at the audience. Every camper was sitting forward now, their eyes glued to Barron's face.

"He knew he should get out of bed and wake up his parents," Barron went on. "Or maybe grab his baseball bat and go after the intruder himself. But he couldn't move! He felt as if he were paralyzed! He just lay there and listened as the footsteps got closer. And closer. And closer. And that's when he noticed that these weren't normal footsteps—thump, thump, thump. They sounded more like thump . . . *draaag*. Thump . . . *draaag*. It was almost as if the person were walking with a limp—the way you would walk . . . if someone had cut off your big toe!

"Just as Grandpa Joe realized that, he heard a voice saying something. He strained to hear the words. As the footsteps got closer, he could just make out the words. 'Who has my big toe?' the voice was muttering."

Barron looked intensely from one face to the next as he mimicked the sound of the moaning voice. "'Who has my big toe?'" he said, his voice getting louder. "'WHO HAS MY BIG TOE?'"

"YOU DO!" someone screamed, jumping out of the bushes and pointing at Tess.

"Aaaggh!" Tess yelled, jumping away from the accusing finger and promptly falling backward off her log.

The audience burst into laughter, both at the sight of Tess lying flat on her back and at Sander, who was grinning broadly at the success of his sudden and dramatic entrance.

"That's so not funny!" Tess pouted as her two bunkmates, Ella Pador and Lorraine Burgess, brushed the dirt off the back of Tess's shirt, trying to calm her down. It didn't work. "This isn't fun, it's life-threatening! I practically had a heart attack!"

"Excellent!" Brown responded. "That's the

sign of a really scary story. Great job, Barron. And Sander, too, of course."

"Hey, no big deal. All I had to do was hide behind that bush until the big finale," Sander said with a shrug.

Mitchie shook her head in admiration. "I've heard that story before, so I was just waiting for Barron to yell the ending," she admitted. "Having someone *else* do it was a great twist."

"Yeah, we're rockin' and rollin' now," Brown said, rubbing his hands together with satisfaction. "So"—he looked around at the other campers—"who's next?"

CHAPTER SIX

There was a brief moment of anticipation as everyone looked at each other. No one wanted to go after Barron's big finale.

"Hey, Shane, I think this is your cue!" Andy called out.

"Yeah, everybody's been talking about your past performance," Torie said, her eyes shining. "Let's hear what all the buzz is about!"

But Shane shook his head, smiling. "Thanks, guys, but I think I need a little more warm-up and inspiration," he said. "I'm sure other people have some great stories to tell. I want to hear those first."

"Well, if you want to hear the best"—Tess jumped to her feet—"I'll go next!"

Ella and Peggy exchanged surprised glances.

"But Tess," Ella said, her forehead wrinkled with confusion, "I thought you just said this wasn't fun."

"Ella!" Tess snapped. "I meant that doing ridiculous things like jumping at people and screaming in their faces isn't fun. My story, on the other hand, will make a shiver go down your spine"—she narrowed her eyes at Sander, who pretended to look abashed—"*without* juvenile attempts to make people scream. And more importantly, my story actually happened to me."

Caitlyn turned and gave Mitchie an

amused smile. Mitchie bit her lip to keep from grinning back. Tess was pretty full of herself, but she definitely had inherited a great talent for performing from her mother. If nothing else, the story should prove to be entertaining. Mitchie quickly grabbed another cookie and settled back to listen.

Sure enough, Tess wasn't satisfied with just sitting on a log and telling her story. Instead, she stood within the circle of firelight, commanding the ground as if she were onstage at Madison Square Garden.

"My story begins on a dark and stormy night in the wilds of Long Island, New York," she said in a low voice. She made a few sweeps of her hands as though that would emphasize the spookiness of her tale. "Rain poured down outside and lightning flashed through the sky as I sat in the living room of the house my mother had rented for the summer while she was putting the final touches on her latest CD."

Mitchie did her best not to roll her eyes. It was nice that Tess was proud of her mom, but did she have to work her superstar connection into everything—even a campfire story? She sighed and tuned back into what Tess was saying.

". . . it was her *Gotta Go Now* album," Tess was saying in a chatty voice, as if she were on a TV talk show. She seemed unaware that the scary atmosphere she'd been trying to create was disappearing as she rambled on. "I remember, because that was the one where Mom had such problems with the third track. The guitar was *completely* overpowering her vocals, and she kept arguing with the engineer about toning it down, but he didn't want to do it. I don't remember why. And so—"

"Um, Tess?" Brown waved a hand in the air to get her attention.

"What?" Tess stared at him haughtily, as if trying to figure out why he had stopped her.

"I think you left us back there on a dark and stormy night," he prompted her.

"Oh." Tess tossed her head, trying to act as if she had meant to go off on a tangent. "Right. I know that. I was just trying to set the scene. So anyway . . . it was a dark and stormy night. The cable had gone out, so I couldn't even watch a music-video channel, and the batteries on my MP3 player had lost their charge. I was completely bored—"

Shane leaned over to whisper to Mitchie, "Now we know why she thinks this is a scary story—no TV and no tunes is the definition of horror for Tess!"

"Brrr," Mitchie whispered back and then giggled. "Goosebumps!"

Tess seemed to sense that she was once again losing her audience. "Anyway," she said firmly, "I was alone in the house"— she paused dramatically—"or at least that's what I thought. As I sat on the couch, reading the latest issue of *Music Review Monthly*,

I heard a strange sound coming from the basement."

"Did it sound something like this?" Andy asked, grinning. "Woooo!"

Tess glared at him. "No, it did not," she said. "It sounded like this." She tilted her head and let out an eerie cry: "*Tessss. Tesssss, where are yoooou?*"

She paused for a moment, and everyone listened as the haunting sound echoed across the lake.

Then an owl hooted as if in answer. Mitchie shivered again, this time for real.

Tess looked around the circle, her eyes gleaming with pleasure as she saw the crowd's reaction. "I didn't want to answer," she went on, "but I couldn't help myself. I felt as if I were in a dream. I stood up from the couch and heard the voice again. *'Tessss, where are yoooou?'* I found myself drawn to the door in the kitchen that led downstairs to the basement. I tried to resist, but I watched as my hand reached out and turned the knob—as if powered by some other force. Without meaning to do it, I started walking down the stairs. As each wooden step creaked under my feet, I wanted to scream, I wanted to turn around and run, but I just couldn't. . . ."

Everyone held their breath, as if caught in the same hypnotic spell that was drawing Tess down to whatever waited for her in the basement. . . .

"Finally, I took the last step onto the cold concrete floor," Tess said, her voice dropping to a whisper. "A chill breeze brushed my cheek and I turned to see a figure draped in white!"

One of the new campers let out a little squeak, then giggled nervously.

"The figure moved toward me, holding out its arms," Tess went on. "A hollow voice rang out as it said, 'There you are! *Finally.*'"

Tess paused, then added, still in a spooky

voice, "*'I told you I wanted your help doing the laundry.'*"

There was a moment's pause as the campers looked at each other in confusion.

"It was my mom," Tess explained as though this was blindingly obvious. "See, she does chores when she's stressed out, and she was holding this sheet up in front of her and—"

She couldn't go on. Her voice was drowned out by the loud booing (and good-natured laughs) that filled the air.

Tess crossed her arms and smirked at her audience. "What?" she asked innocently. "You said you wanted a terrifying tale . . . and what's more terrifying than housework?"

CHAPTER SEVEN

After Tess's story, Brown declared a s'mores and popcorn break to, as he said, "call down the magical mojo of more ferociously frightening tales of terror!"

Soon the night was filled with singing as groups broke into typical campfire tunes. The kids who weren't singing swarmed to get the fixings for s'mores.

As Mitchie pulled a gooey and singed

marshmallow from her stick and carefully placed it between two graham crackers, Torie edged over to her.

"Hey, there," she said brightly.

Mitchie glanced up and felt her good mood dim a bit. But she didn't want to be unwelcoming. "Hey, you're Torie, right?" she said. The other girl nodded. When she didn't offer more, Mitchie introduced herself and then asked, "How do you like the Scary Story Bonfire so far?"

"Oh, it's totally cool," Torie said, wide-eyed. "And Camp Rock is so awesome! I've dreamed of coming here for years and now that I finally made it, well . . ." Her voice trailed off and she gave a slightly embarrassed laugh. "Well, sometimes I can't believe it's real."

Mitchie warmed toward Torie in spite of herself. "Oh, I know," she said with feeling. "I used to wake up every morning and think, hey, maybe I was just dreaming—"

Before Mitchie could finish, Torie's gaze

moved away from her and her smile widened. "Oh, hi, Shane!" she said brightly. "Hey, I wanted to tell you I really loved that set you did at B-Note. Your new songs sound really cool."

"Thanks," Shane said. He moved from behind Mitchie and held out a water. "Hey, Mitchie, I thought you might want one of these. The cooler's almost empty."

Mitchie took the water with a smile of thanks, but it was forced. She could see Torie out of the corner of her eye, glancing back and forth from Mitchie to Shane.

And Mitchie knew exactly what Torie was thinking. She was thinking about how lucky Mitchie was to be good friends with Shane. She was thinking that this was what Camp Rock was all about, making connections. And she was thinking that the people you met meant more than your hard work or your talent or your drive. . . .

"Looks like you need some chocolate on

that s'more," Shane said.

"What?" Mitchie shook her head, trying to snap out of her worries.

He pointed at the graham-cracker-and-marshmallow sandwich she was holding. "It's not any good without the chocolate," he said.

"Oh, yeah," she said. "Right."

But as Mitchie looked down at her snack, she felt her heart sink. Suddenly, the fun had vanished, and she no longer felt like having a treat.

"**H**ey, everybody!" Andy yelled. "Get a load of this!" He was holding a set of bongo drums between his knees. He raised his hands high and then brought them down to play a few fast beats. The percussive sound echoed through the woods.

Immediately, the campers settled down.

"Sounds like you're ready to tell the next story," Brown said.

"You bet," Andy said. There was a light

smattering of applause, but he held up his hand and everyone quieted down.

"My story begins in a small town in Ireland called Kircastle," Andy said. "A girl named Mary lived there, as well as a boy named Sean. Mary and Sean had grown up together and had been best friends their whole lives. They liked to do a lot of the same things—having picnics on the beach, hiking in the hills around Kircastle—but there were two activities they disagreed on.

"Mary loved to dance. She loved going to music clubs for teens and doing the latest dance moves, but she'd also agree, in a pinch, to go to the little pub in Kircastle when local musicians played and everyone danced traditional Irish jigs.

"Sean, on the other hand, hated to dance," Andy went on. "If Mary ever did convince him to come along, he usually sat against the wall, his arms folded, and just listened to the music."

"He wouldn't fit in at Camp Rock then," Barron called out.

There were hoots of laughter at this, but Andy shook his head.

"Actually, he would be right at home here," he said. "Because Sean was . . . a drummer!"

He hit his drum a few times with a flourish, and everyone applauded.

"Sean also loved everything concerning Irish folklore. He enjoyed listening to the old stories about the fairy folk in Ireland," Andy went on. "He even learned to play the bodhran, the Irish pan drum, and sometimes he would play along as Mary danced. But Mary just laughed when he told what she called his 'wee fairy stories.' When he was finished, she always insisted that they go to the center of town and buy some CDs. She was only interested in the latest pop or rock."

"Smart girl!" Caitlyn said. "Sounds like she wants to keep on top of the newest sounds."

"Spoken like a true producer," Mitchie said teasingly.

Caitlyn shrugged and grinned. "What can I say? I'm always thinking about the business."

"*Anyway*," Andy said pointedly, "as I was saying . . ."

"We're on the edges of our seats," Caitlyn said, waving a hand at him to go on.

"Mary and Sean kept arguing about their two points of view," Andy said. "Mary would tell Sean why she loved hip-hop"—he pounded out a quick hip-hop beat on his drum—"and Sean would counter with why he loved Irish folk music." He did a quick drumroll, then said, "One fine summer evening, Sean asked Mary to go for a walk. He carried his drum as they walked through the warm twilight to a small hill outside the village.

"Sean suggested that they sit down on the grass at the base of the hill. When they were settled, he started playing his drum, softly at first"—Andy gently tapped his fingers on the

77

drum—"then louder and faster." Andy kept drumming, increasing the tempo and volume until the woods rang with the percussive sound.

Mitchie felt herself moving along to the beat.

Then Andy dramatically stopped drumming and looked around the circle. "After a short time, both Sean and Mary fell asleep. When they woke up, they were no longer on the hill outside their village. They were in a vast hall, shining with candles and gold. Dozens of strange people—tall, beautiful, and unearthly looking—surrounded them. Sean didn't need to think twice to know that these people were not human. One of them, a young man, stepped forward and held out his hand to Mary.

" 'Will you dance with me?' he asked. Then he turned to Sean. 'And will you play?'

"Sean nodded, unable to speak. He felt that he had been struck dumb. As he looked around at the brilliant company, he remembered that it was Midsummer's Eve. And he knew what he was seeing. He and Mary had been transported into a hall under the hill, where the fairy folk gathered to dance and celebrate the longest day of the year."

Andy paused, letting the silence stretch out. Then, very softly, he began beating out a rhythm on his drum. "Sean began to play," he said. "Somewhere in the crowd, a piper joined in, and then another. Soon, music was swirling through the cavernous room, and Mary was swept off in the dance."

As he spoke, Andy kept drumming, building the intensity of the sound as he went on. "Sean had read many stories about the fairy folk, and he knew one important thing: if you were ever lucky—or unlucky—enough to find your way into a fairy hall, you should never eat a bite of food or take a sip of drink. If you did, you would never be able to return to the human world.

"So Sean played his drum, but he kept an eye on Mary. When the dance ended, he saw Mary being ushered over to a banquet table.

"As she reached forward, smiling, to take a small cake, Sean stopped drumming.

"When she lifted the cake to her mouth, he jumped to his feet.

"And when she opened her lips to take a bite, he ran over to her.

"'No!' Sean yelled. 'Mary! Stop!'

"Startled, she jumped and turned to him. He grabbed the cake out of her hand and shoved it into his coat pocket. There was a murmur of disappointment and anger from the fairy folk. Sean also knew from the legends he had read that very few humans had ever escaped from the fairies, and that they could be cruel when they didn't get their way. Sean knew that he and Mary had to get out of there, fast.

"He grabbed Mary's hand and yelled in her

ear, 'Come on, Mary! Run!' Pulling her behind him, he raced through the crowd, heading toward what looked like a door."

Andy began hitting his drum in a fast, staccato beat. He raised his voice in volume and urgency. "When they reached the door, Sean saw a hall and turned down it. As they ran, Mary gasped, 'Sean, where are we going? What's wrong?'

"'Don't ask questions,' he replied. 'Just keep running!'"

Andy was really pounding on his drum now, increasing the tempo of the story. "The fairy folk were right behind them, moaning and crying with disappointment. Sean tried to run even faster, but he was having trouble breathing. Mary tripped, and they lost precious seconds as he helped her up. They kept running, and then . . . he smelled a fresh summer breeze.

"A few seconds later, Sean and Mary burst out of the tunnel and onto the hillside. They stood still for a few minutes in the cool night air, catching their breath.

"Mary looked at Sean. 'Thanks,' she said.

" 'No problem,' he answered. He reached into his coat pocket for the cake, meaning to throw it away. But all he found was a handful of dried leaves and berries.

"Sean's eyes met Mary's.

" 'Did that even happen?' she asked.

"He shrugged. 'I don't know,' he said. 'But let's go get a cup of tea.' "

Andy grinned. Then, with a flourish of a drumroll between each word, he added, "And that . . . is . . . the . . . end."

Applause and cheers filled the air.

"Great job, Andy," Caitlyn said. "I can't believe you figured out how to work in some drumming."

"Hey, percussion makes everything more dramatic," Andy said. "And I thought even if you guys didn't like my story, you'd at least listen to the bongos." He took a sip of water, then pointed his bottle at Shane. "Speaking of stories, though, I think it's time to hear the master storyteller!"

"Yes, I've been waiting for this all night!" Tess said.

"Doesn't anybody else want a turn?" Shane said. "I can wait."

"No, you can't!" Ella yelled.

Barron and Sander started a chant: "Shane! Shane! Shane!"

Brown shook his head, grinning. "If there's one thing I learned in the music business, it's always give the crowd what they want! Take the stage, Shane!"

"Okay, okay," Shane said. "Here we go. . . ."

CHAPTER EIGHT

"**M**y story begins many years ago, on a dark night in Mississippi," Shane began, "but it ends right here at Camp Rock."

Mitchie glanced around the campfire and saw that everyone's eyes had brightened at the connection. It would only make the story that much spookier.

"I hope you're not going to tell us there's a ghost in our cabin," Ella said with a dramatic shiver. "I won't get a wink if I hear that."

"Woo-ooo-ooo." Barron made a spooky sound as Sander laughed.

"Pay no attention to the comedians by the fire," Shane said with a lofty wave of his hand. "This is not a tale of terror, but of mystery. As I said, it started a long time ago, in the 1920s, in fact. There was a guitar player named Sam Jackson who lived in the Mississippi Delta. He wanted more than anything to be the best blues player in the world. But unfortunately, he wasn't.

"He played and played until his fingers were sore. He played for his family when the day's work was done. He played for his friends and neighbors at barn dances and harvest festivals. He was a cheerful man and everyone liked him, but they had to admit that his playing was, at best, average."

Shane took a deep breath before continuing. "But then one day, Sam heard a mysterious story about an old woman who lived in the woods by a creek, with only her cat, a cow, and a few chickens for company. Everyone who lived in those parts was afraid of her. Some even said she was a witch. But Sam was smart enough not to believe that. In fact, he felt sorry for her living all alone like that.

"One day it started raining, a real downpour. It rained for three days straight. Rivers overflowed their banks, houses and barns were flooded, and a few trees were even swept away in the rushing water.

"Sam started worrying about the old woman. Finally, when the rain and flooding had eased, he decided to check on her. When he got to her house, he found her sitting on the roof with her chickens and her cat. The cow had apparently retreated to the top of a hill and made its way home later that day.

"After Sam helped the old woman down, she thanked him and invited him to have a cup of tea. As always, he was carrying his guitar with him so that he could practice whenever he had a spare moment. The old woman asked him to play and for a while, the only sound was his strumming as she listened. When Sam finally stopped she said, 'You have the heart to play music.'

"Sam nodded, and the old woman went on, 'I suppose, like most people, you also want riches and fame.'

"But Sam shook his head. 'No,' he said. 'All I want to do is play the music I can hear in my head and feel in my heart.' He hesitated, then added sadly, 'I hear it so clear and pure. But somehow I can't get my fingers to follow along.'

"She smiled. 'That's the right answer. You've done me a good turn today, so I'll do one for you in return. Tonight the moon will be bright. Take your guitar to the crossroads outside town and stand in the moonlight as the hour strikes midnight—and you will have your heart's desire.'"

Shane paused and smiled at the hush that

had fallen over the campfire. He brushed a few strands of brown hair out of his eyes, then went on. "Well, Sam thanked her for the advice and swore that he would follow it. But once he left the old woman to go home, he started having second thoughts. It sounded like a pretty crazy idea, after all. What kind of magic could there be in moonlight at midnight? As he thought those words, he could hear how they would sound if set to music. He even heard the tune! He started working on the song, trying to add more lyrics, trying to find the melody . . . but, as usual, he had no luck.

"Then darkness fell. He sat by the fire, strumming his guitar and thinking about how much he wanted to play better. As it got later and later, he started having *third* thoughts.

"'What could it hurt?' he asked himself. 'No one will ever know, so no one can laugh at me if it doesn't work.' So, his mind made up, he picked up his guitar and headed for the crossroads without telling anybody."

"Ooh, this is getting kind of spooky," Caitlyn murmured to Mitchie.

"Shh, it's also getting really good," Mitchie whispered back. She could see where the story was going, of course. She was sure everybody could. But what was the connection between this bluesman and Camp Rock? She couldn't wait to find out.

As if Shane sensed Mitchie's thoughts, he looked at her and smiled. Then he turned back toward the fire. As the light flickered across his handsome face, he went on, his voice hushed: "It was a dark night. The moon was full, but it was hidden behind a thick layer of clouds. By the time Sam got to the crossroads, he worried that he was too late. He stood there for what felt like forever—and then he heard it. The sound of the church clock striking the hour. As he counted to twelve, the moon came out from behind the clouds and spilled silver light across the land. Sam held his guitar up until the clock stopped chiming.

"When the last note had died away, he felt, somewhere deep inside him, that he had changed. Or maybe the guitar had changed. Or maybe both. He headed home, tired but happy.

"He didn't dare play his guitar again until the next day. He went out into the fields in the morning, the way he always did. He worked hard all day, the way he always did. He sat on his porch after supper with his guitar in his lap, the way he always did. And then a few friends stopped by. They talked for a bit, then he asked if they wanted him to play for them.

"And, as they always did, because they were his friends, they said yes. And when he did . . . everyone, including Sam, was astonished! He played like no one they had ever heard before. Every note sang out clearly. His fingers danced over the strings.

When he played a cheerful tune, people couldn't help but dance. When he played a sad one, they couldn't help but cry.

"Sam went on to live a long life and, to the end of his days, he did nothing but play his guitar. He never made a lot of money, and no one outside the Delta knew his name, but his dream of giving voice to the music he heard in his head had finally come true. And then, after he died . . ."

"Oh, no, this is the ghost part, isn't it?" Ella moaned. "Is Sam haunting Camp Rock?" She glanced nervously over her shoulder. "I'm going to be afraid to walk back to the cabin now, aren't I?"

"No worries," Brown said. "If there were a ghost hanging around this camp, I think I'd know about it. And I'd be proud to have someone like Sam here. In fact, I think we'd have to make him an honorary camper."

"Come on, Shane!" Andy yelled. "Let us know how it ends!"

"Well, as I was saying, after a long and happy life, Sam passed away," Shane said. "And somehow, when his few possessions were passed on, the guitar was . . . *lost!*"

"What?" Mitchie said. "How could anyone lose a magic guitar?"

Shane laughed. "It wasn't magic, exactly. But it was certainly gone. And no one knew where it was. Until one day . . ."

He let the silence stretch out until Barron and Sander pelted him with marshmallows.

"Okay, okay," he finally said, holding up his hands in surrender. "No one saw the guitar again until fifty years later, when it ended up being sold in an auction, along with a bunch of old farm equipment, rusty pots and pans, and moth-eaten bedspreads."

"How did it end up there?" Torie asked.

"Who knows?" Shane shrugged. "That's part of the mystery. Anyway, it went up for auction and was bought for only about ten bucks . . . by one of the original Camp Rockers."

"Really?" Mitchie asked, amazed despite the fact that Shane had told them the story found its way to Camp Rock.

"How cool!" Caitlyn cried.

"Is the guitar here somewhere?" Barron asked.

"Yeah, it should be in a glass case or something," Sander added.

"I want to see it," Ella said.

"I want to *play* it," Tess said.

"Whoa, whoa," Shane said. "Here's the thing. The guitar was at Camp Rock for almost a week and then . . . it disappeared again."

"No!" everybody yelled.

"Sorry, dudes," Shane said, but he was grinning. "It's gone. Or . . . is it?"

His listeners quieted down immediately. For a long moment, all they could hear were the logs crackling in the fire and a gentle breeze blowing through the leaves on the trees. Then, very softly, Shane said, "You see, even though the *guitar* was gone, people still claimed to feel its presence."

"How?" Mitchie asked softly.

"After a while, stories started circulating," Shane explained. "Every once in a while, a camper would go out for a walk late at night. And sometimes they would end up in that clearing by the lake—you know, the one where the big boulder and the crooked pine tree are?"

Everyone nodded in unison.

"And if they happened to be there at midnight when the moon is bright, some of them claimed they heard the sound of a blues guitar playing softly," Shane said in a quiet voice. "But here's the thing . . . not everyone can hear it. The legend is that the only people who can hear Sam's guitar are the ones who are *true* musicians."

He turned to look into Mitchie's eyes

and added, "If you hear the guitar playing at midnight, you know you're one of the musicians with true soul."

And with that, Shane's story came to an end.

CHAPTER NINE

Brown let the silence stretch out for a moment after Shane had finished. While Shane's story might not have been the scariest, there was no doubt that he had earned his reputation. Finally, Brown stood up, breaking the spell.

"Okay, campers, that's a wrap!" he yelled, clapping his hands. "Great job, everybody. The stories were awesome, and I, for one, will not sleep well tonight."

The campers laughed and applauded before wandering off toward their cabins, chatting quietly.

"Well?" Caitlyn asked Mitchie as they headed home. "What did you think of your first Scary Story Bonfire at Camp Rock?"

"It was fantastic," Mitchie said, but her voice was flat and far away.

Caitlyn gave her a curious sidelong glance. Mitchie was clearly lost in her own thoughts.

"Are you okay?" Caitlyn asked.

"Oh, sure," Mitchie said more brightly. "Just a little tired, I guess."

Before Caitlyn could pursue this, they were overtaken by Torie and her friends Jessie and Sallie Jo.

"Wow, that's one camp tradition that definitely lived up to all the hype," Torie said. "And Shane's story was definitely the best."

"Oh, thank you *very* much," Barron said,

pretending to be upset. He had been walking a few feet in front of the girls with Sander and Andy. The three of them waited for the group of girls to catch up.

"No, dude, she's right," Andy said. "You and Sander scared everybody—"

"And your drumming was awesome," Jessie added.

"But let's face it," Andy finished, "Shane still holds the prize for best story. That Camp Rock connection? Totally jammin'!"

There was a murmur of agreement.

Then Torie said, very casually, "So, Mitchie, speaking of jammin'—are you going to sing a new song at this week's jam session?"

"Um, yeah, I think so," Mitchie said, hoping that her voice didn't sound as uncertain as she felt.

"I'm sure it will be great," Torie said. "Hey, maybe Shane will sing it on his new CD! That would be a big break for you, wouldn't it?"

Mitchie did her best not to glare at Torie. "I don't think it's really Shane's style," she said evenly. "And anyway, I still have to finish it."

Torie exchanged a knowing glance with her friends Jessie and Sallie Jo. "I'm sure you'll finish it," she said, "and I'm sure Shane will *love* it. No matter what style it is."

Mitchie felt her face flush. This was ridiculous. "Really," she said sharply, unable to hold in her emotions any longer. "Well, I'm not so sure I'll be able to write the song I hear in my head. And if I can't, Shane will never get a chance to say whether he thinks it's any good or not."

Turning, she stomped into her cabin, still seething. A few minutes later, Caitlyn entered.

"Um, Mitchie?" Caitlyn asked. "Are you *sure* you're okay? Cause, um, you are not really *acting*, okay."

"Oh, yeah, sure," Mitchie said with a sigh.

She flopped back on her bed and stared at the ceiling. "I'm sorry I blew up out there. It's just that I don't like it when people think that I'm planning to get ahead by hitching my star to Shane's wagon."

Caitlyn grinned as she stretched out on her own bed. "You're not still worried about that, are you?"

Mitchie's eyes slid sideways. "Of course not," she said.

Caitlyn met her gaze and, after a few seconds, they both burst out laughing. Mitchie was totally caught.

"I know! I'm supersensitive. But Torie's comments really got under my skin," Mitchie admitted. "I can't help it! I've been trying to let it go all day, the way you said I should, and it's just not working."

Caitlyn rolled over onto her stomach. "You know what you need to do?" she asked, suddenly serious. "You need to finish that song. That's really what has made you so on edge.

You're questioning yourself because you're stuck. But if you had a breakthrough—which you will, Mitchie, 'cause you always do!—you wouldn't think twice about all that silly gossip."

Mitchie gave her friend a grateful glance and nodded. "You're right," she said. "So, do you mind if I work for a while? I don't want my light to bother you—"

Caitlyn gave her a careless wave. "Not a problem," she said breezily. "I've only got two chapters to go in my book, and I'm just getting to the exciting part! Stay up with your light on as late as you want. I'll be up with ya!"

But two hours later, Caitlyn was fast asleep, the novel open on her stomach. Mitchie glanced over at her friend, who was snoring quietly, and grinned. She had just spent two hours racking her brain, trying to figure out what her melody needed, scribbling all kinds of lyrics in her notebook . . . and so far she still hadn't come up with anything that worked.

Still, the sight of her friend, who had been so encouraging, made Mitchie realize how lucky she was.

Caitlyn doesn't care if I'm a huge success or just another frustrated songwriter, she thought as she turned out her light and pulled her blanket up to her chin. Neither does my mom. Or my dad. In fact, all the people who really love me think I'm great, whether I get a song recorded or win a Grammy or end up writing songs that no one will ever hear. . . .

Still, as she closed her eyes and tried to relax so she could go to sleep, Mitchie found that her mind was racing.

What is wrong with me? she wondered. I've never had such problems with a song before. Never!

As she stared into the darkness, unable to sleep, she found herself remembering Shane's story. She knew it was just for fun, but still, it echoed in her heart and mind, especially now, when she was so full of doubts about herself and her skills.

What would it be like to hear the guitar playing in the moonlight?

What it would be like to know that she was on the right track, that she was going to be a successful artist?

What would it be like to be reassured that she would be known someday for her song-writing talent, not just for being Shane's friend?

These thoughts ran through Mitchie's mind, until suddenly she knew what she had to do. She threw back her quilt and got out of bed, moving quietly so she wouldn't wake Caitlyn.

Quickly, she pulled on khaki shorts and a T-shirt, then thrust her feet into a pair of beat-up old sneakers. With one backward glance at her sleeping friend, she eased her way out the door and tiptoed down the steps. Once she reached the path that led into the woods, she started running.

The moon was high in the black sky, lighting her way. Her heart pounding, Mitchie headed for the clearing. A quick glance at her watch told her that she had fifteen minutes until midnight.

A part of her knew Shane's story wasn't true, but still Mitchie ran, until the pounding of her feet drowned out all her thoughts. There was no turning back now.

CHAPTER
TEN

When Mitchie arrived at the clearing, however, all her doubts quickly returned. She sat on the boulder under the crooked pine tree and rested for a moment, trying to catch her breath. What am I doing? she thought. I never do anything this impulsive—or silly.

As she sat quietly, her heartbeat gradually slowing to a normal pace, she became aware of the way the moonlight fell on the grass and of how still the night was. Even the breeze had died down.

She tilted her head back and looked up at the stars. Since coming to Camp Rock, she had discovered that she loved spotting constellations in the night sky. The stars were so much brighter here than they were at home, so finding the Big Dipper and Orion seemed much easier.

And when she was feeling upset about something—such as a song that just wasn't working—looking at the stars helped her see the problem as a relatively minor annoyance that she would be able to handle, one way or the other.

Tonight, however, the stars were not helping her. In fact, the longer she looked at them, the smaller she felt.

Maybe, Mitchie thought, Torie and her friends were right.

Mitchie knew she had a talent for songwriting—but was it, perhaps, a rather *small* talent? Was she fooling herself into thinking that she could make it as a songwriter and an artist even without her friendship with Shane?

She hated to think that, but if she was being honest with herself, she knew that what Torie and her friends had said contained a kernel of truth—a lot of famous people became successful because they had the right connections.

Mitchie's mind turned once again to Shane's story. Now that she thought about it, didn't the legend of Sam's guitar kind of prove Torie's point? Poor old Sam. He may have been an amazing blues guitarist, but he didn't even know enough to network with big music stars or powerful producers! True, he must have been a really nice guy to help that old woman, and he had been given an amazing gift in return. But then he didn't know how to take advantage of it, so he had lived his life as a complete unknown.

She sat still for a moment, feeling sad for Sam and wondering if Shane's story was true. Could Sam's spirit really live on here at Camp Rock? In a mysterious—and missing— guitar? Then her thoughts were interrupted by a noise somewhere behind her. She jumped to her feet before realizing that all she had heard was a pinecone falling to the ground.

Get a grip on yourself, Mitchie, she thought, grinning slightly. Next thing you know, you'll be imagining that Sam's ghost has come back to haunt you!

She glanced at her watch. It was seven minutes until midnight. Now that she was here, hanging out in the woods instead of sleeping in her cozy bed, she was beginning to feel rather chilly. She wished time would go by a little faster.

It just shows that Shane really is a great storyteller, she thought, standing up and brushing traces of dirt off her clothes. He totally had me convinced that I would get some kind of secret message about my talent if I traipsed out here in the dead of night!

For a moment, she considered whether the next day she should tell him what she had done. . . . Then she shook her head. No, it was time to go. She started to walk quickly out of the clearing and down the dark, wooded path.

Shane would just laugh at how gullible she was if she told him about this. Plus then she'd have to tell him the reason she went in the first place. And she definitely wouldn't want anyone else at Camp Rock to find out she had actually headed for the clearing, hoping to have some kind of mystical encounter. After all, she was certainly the only camper who was gullible enough to believe Shane's story . . .

Then Mitchie ran headlong into a dark figure standing in the middle of the path. It seemed to have appeared without warning, as if it had formed from the shadows, and Mitchie felt her heart skip a beat.

"Aagghh!" Mitchie screamed

"Aagghh!" Whoever—or *whatever* it was—screamed back.

For a split second, Mitchie wondered wildly if this was a ghost, maybe even the ghost of Sam . . . and then her reason returned.

Whoever she had just run into was solidly human, dressed in shorts and a hoodie, and smelled of expensive perfume.

Furthermore, the "ghost's" scream was instantly followed by an exasperated voice saying, "What are *you* doing here?"

"Oh, Tess, it's you," Mitchie said. "Well, I'm guessing I'm here for the same reason you are. Come on."

They headed back to the clearing. Once they were standing in the moonlight, Mitchie added, "You were cutting it kind of close, weren't you? I mean, it's almost midnight."

"I don't know what you mean," Tess said huffily. "I couldn't sleep, that's all."

"Uh-huh." Mitchie crossed her arms and waited while Tess bit her lip and stared at the ground.

Finally, Tess threw up her hands in surrender. "Okay, okay," she said. "Even though I know Shane made up that whole story, I admit it—I wanted to find out just how good I really am."

She tossed her blond hair and lifted her chin an inch. "I mean, I *know* I'm going to be a star one day, but I would like to know exactly how enormously famous I'll end up being."

A faint crease appeared between Mitchie's brows. "Um, Tess?" she said. "Did you listen to the whole story?"

"Of course I did!" Tess said. "Well, most of it."

"You missed the whole point!" Mitchie said. "Sam didn't end up famous at all."

"What? He *didn't*?" Tess's eyes widened, then narrowed in suspicion. "Look, my attention may have drifted a little bit after that man got his magical powers or whatever, but I'm *sure* that at the end Shane said that anyone who hears the guitar is supposed to be a great musician."

"*A musician with soul,*" Mitchie corrected her. "Which may mean that you play music your whole life just for the joy of playing music."

There was a long pause while Tess looked at Mitchie with astonishment. "You mean, not be famous?" she asked. "Not be a star?"

"Well, you might end up as a star, but you might not," Mitchie answered. "See, it wouldn't really matter, because—"

She didn't get to finish.

"Never mind!" Tess interrupted. "I've already lost too much beauty sleep as it is. And anyway"—she glanced nervously over her shoulder—"I'm not sure I like this place at night. I keep hearing weird little sounds."

"It's probably just the wind," Mitchie said. "But you're right, everything sounds spookier in the dark."

Just then, there was a rustling noise a few feet away, as if a small animal was scurrying through fallen leaves. Tess jumped, then tried to pretend she hadn't.

"All right, I'm out of here," she said quickly. "What about you?"

Mitchie shook her head. Suddenly leaving didn't feel like the right choice. "I think I'll watch the stars for a little bit longer," she said. "See you in the morning, Tess."

"See you," Tess said as she hurried back down the path.

Mitchie resumed sitting on the boulder, happy to be alone again. She was surprisingly glad that Tess had kept her from going.

When Mitchie had talked about the importance of playing music just for the joy of it, she really heard her own words for the first time . . . and, she knew that they were true.

She stretched her arms over her head and smiled up at the stars. So what if Shane's story was just make-believe? she thought. It still did what it was supposed to do.

And just then, Mitchie heard a new sound from somewhere deep in the forest. The faint notes of a blues song being plucked on an old guitar . . .

Mitchie sat up straight. She caught her breath as a chill ran up her spine.

No, she thought in disbelief. It can't be true. It *can't* be.

Then she heard a sound, like footsteps walking through the woods, and a figure moved among the trees. It was carrying a guitar. The blues song got louder as the figure headed in her direction, getting closer, and closer, and closer . . .

Goosebumps appeared on Mitchie's arms

as she watched the guitar player approach. She wanted to scream, but she couldn't find her voice. She wanted to run, but she felt as if she'd been turned to stone. And she wanted, more than anything else, to be back in her own bed, safe and sound, but that was no longer an option. . . .

"Hey, Mitchie."

The guitar player stepped into the clearing.

Mitchie blinked. There stood Shane, the moonlight falling on his dark hair.

"I hope I didn't scare you," he said, smiling sheepishly.

She cleared her throat and took a deep breath. "Of course not," she said, as lightly as she could. "I knew it was you all along."

His smile widened. "Oh, good. Because, you know, you looked kind of frightened."

"Well, I wasn't!" she said quickly. "Not at all." Then she caught the gleam in his eyes and started to laugh. "Well. Maybe just a *little.*"

Shane came over to sit next to her, propping the guitar on the boulder. "Sorry," he said. "My intentions were good."

Mitchie leaned sideways, the better to look into his face. "Really? What *were* your intentions, anyway? And how did you know I would turn up?"

He shrugged. "I didn't know for sure," he admitted, "but I thought the odds were pretty good. You've been kind of preoccupied lately, and, well, I thought maybe you needed some encouragement. . . ." His voice trailed off.

Mitchie gave him a knowing look.

"What?" he asked.

"You talked to Caitlyn, didn't you?" she said.

"What? Me? Caitlyn? No!" he protested.

Laughing, she shook her head. "Don't even try it, Shane."

He tried to look innocent for a few more seconds, and then gave it up with a sheepish shrug. "Sorry," he said. "I was just worried about you. So when Caitlyn said you were upset about a song that was giving you trouble—"

Mitchie gave him a sharp look. "Is that all she said?"

"Of course," he said, puzzled. "That seemed like enough. I know how much you care about your music."

"It means everything to me," she said simply. Inside, she felt relief. She should have known Caitlyn would never tell Shane that Mitchie was worried about how other people saw their friendship.

"So then I remembered this old folk tale I heard once about a blues player down South, and I thought the theme was perfect. . . ."

"Oh, yes?" Mitchie refocused on what Shane was saying.

"Yeah, and I figured out a way to add a Camp Rock twist," he went on. "I hoped you would want to test it out. Of course, I didn't count on Tess getting the same idea—although I guess I should have expected that!"

They both laughed, then Shane picked up the guitar and began playing it softly.

"Nice tune," Mitchie said.

"Thanks," he said.

She started humming along, adding some harmony, then riffing on the melody.

He followed her lead, improvising on where she took the melody, then sliding into yet another variation.

Mitchie watched the moonbeams dreamily as she and Shane wove the song together. She felt something inside her loosen, and she knew that this feeling was what she had been searching for. This sense of relaxation and joy was all she needed to write her songs.

When they finally finished, they looked at each other with pleased surprise . . . and just a little nervousness.

"I know you made up that story, Shane,"

Mitchie whispered. "But I really do think—"

He nodded as if he had read her mind. "That old Sam is here with us right now?" he whispered back. "Yeah. I think so, too."

"So maybe we should just, um . . ." She tilted her head toward the path.

"Go back to our cabins?" he finished, even as he was standing up and taking her hand. "I totally agree."

They quickly headed back through the woods without saying a word.

But back in the clearing, when Mitchie and Shane were already too far away to hear, a few blues notes shimmered through the air, then gradually faded away into the night.

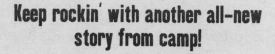

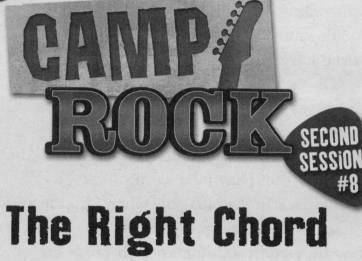

The Right Chord

By James Ponti

Based on "Camp Rock," Written by Karin Gist & Regina Hicks and Julie Brown & Paul Brow

For as long as she could remember, Mitchie
Torres dreamed of being a performing artist
like the ones she saw on Hot Tunes. And for
as long as she could remember, that dream

seemed like a farfetched fantasy. But, at the start of summer her mother did an amazing thing. Connie Torres got a job as the cook at Camp Rock, making it possible for Mitchie to go where she could eat, drink and live music twenty-four hours a day.

Now, on the last day of camp, the fantasy no longer seemed so farfetched. Mitchie was about to sing a duet with Colby Miller, one of her new friends from camp, in the Parents Concert.

As was tradition, the Parents Concert was the last of the summer. It was a chance for the campers to show their parents what they had learned and Mitchie wanted to show her mother how much all of this had meant to her. Right before the song started, she looked out into the audience and saw her. Both smiled.

The music began and Mitchie and Colby felt it from their fingers to their toes. The mood of the evening flowed into the song and when Mitchie held the final note as the music trailed off, the entire audience jumped to its feet and gave them a standing ovation.

It felt amazing. Mitchie wished she could bottle up the moment and keep it forever.

"You were great!" Colby cried.

"So were you," Mitchie said, grinning. "You nailed those high notes."

As they smiled and waved at the still applauding audience, Mitchie was filled with excitement about the performance but also sadness because it was all coming to an end.

"I don't know about you," Colby said leaning over so she could hear him over the audience. "But I need some water. It's hot up here."

Mitchie was hot and thirsty too, but part of her didn't want to leave the stage. She closed her eyes and tried to freeze the moment in her memory. She wanted to remember exactly how this felt. After a couple seconds she opened them back up and turned to Colby and nodded.

"I'm thirsty too. Let's get out of here."

They waved to the crowd one last time and headed backstage as the next act was coming on to get ready.

The first person to greet them was Shane Gray who gave Colby a high five and then locked eyes with Mitchie.

"Your voice is amazing," he said. "That's the only word for it. Amazing."

Something about Shane's eyes made Mitchie forget how hot and thirsty she was. Those eyes also made her forget about all of the noise and other people that were around them. She imagined that as the lead singer of the super famous band, Connect Three, those eyes did that to a lot of girls. Still . . . he was her friend and that meant a lot.

"Thanks!" she managed to reply as she tried to catch her breath.

Mitchie didn't get to admire Shane's eyes for long, because it was only a matter of seconds before Caitlyn was there with a couple bottles of ice cold water. She tossed one to Colby, who started chugging it instantly.

Caitlyn gave her review in a single word. Actually it was four words, but she said them so fast they seemed like one. "Absolutely-Unbelievably-Incredibly-Awesome!"

Mitchie laughed and took a gulp of the water. She couldn't believe that this had become a part of her life. Before the summer started, she had been a shy kid who wrote songs in secret because she didn't think they were good enough for others to hear. And now she was sharing them with dozens of friends. Life couldn't get much sweeter.